Seoı
A Sh

MW00937484

By, T.A. Walker

Copyright© 2019
T. A. Walker

All rights reserved. No part of this book may be reproduced in any form, or by any electronic or mechanical means, including information storage and retrieval systems, without permission in writing from the publishers, except by a reviewer who may quote brief passages in a review.

Publisher: Kindle Direct Publishing

The characters and events in this book are fictitious. Any similarity to real persons, living or dead, is coincidental and not intended by the author.

January 2

I remember sitting in George's office. He claimed that I needed to let the world in. I remember begging him not to send me anywhere but back to the studio in LA. Yet, I still don't know how I got here. I can't move off the living room floor of my studio apartment in South Korea.

I can hear George telling me that a month with Burn It Up will do my career some good. He says that American Idol showed the world that I have the It factor, now I have to prove it. His advice would be good if he could prove to me that he's not stealing every dime I make. He controls my life. I have nothing unless he gives it to me. Even the allergy pills I've been overdosing on came from him.

He couldn't have picked a worse place to send me, but what I want doesn't matter. What George says goes, so I'm here.

A car will be here any minute, but I'd rather sleep. I'm not in the mood to do any of this. Especially this. These guys look so good, that I'm nervous for them to see my flaws. Their skin shines on camera. And not the oily skin I have. No, they have dewy supple skin that I couldn't begin to know how to get. Their eye makeup looks better on them than anything I've ever had. Maybe if I can learn their beauty tips this trip won't be so bad. George promises that I'll have the stylist soon. It takes time he always says right after he says no to one of my requests.

BIU is a mixed bag of talent. Ranging from rappers to singers, and dancers. When George explained to me that they do it all, I figured that he was being lazy as usual, but he wasn't lying. On any given song, it's hard to know what to expect. The more videos I saw, the more I needed to see. When I finally remembered to turn on the English captions, I could not put the phone down.

By the time I was being shuttled off the plane, I felt like I knew the members. In twelve hours, I also knew that I was a fan, something I've never allowed myself to do. I've loved bands, yes, but being a fan is something different. After seeing Ji, dance and sing to me for twelve hours, it was hard to deny that I was in. All in. But that didn't change my wanting to spend a month in his country. I, like millions of girls around the world, could have been content binging on their videos. But this, this is intimidating. Even though his hair is lavender like a flower, and his clothes are attention-grabbing, he's all man. And I don't know how the duality of his persona pulls it off. Any man who can look good with hair the color of a crayon on any given day deserves the kind of attention Ji gets. This isn't how I would want to meet them though. I would want to be on my stomping grounds. A place where I had the advantage of the culture and language. This set up has me feeling like a duck out of water. I don't feel comfortable in my own skin, and I don't know what to do to find my confidence.

American Idol never should have happened to me. I entered the contest as a desperate joke. The love that I wanted, didn't want me, so I was immune to rejection. I figured that not making it on American Idol couldn't hurt any more than losing my mom and boyfriend in the same year. That was five years ago, and I'm still as surprised by my supposed success as the interviewers are.

Watching a million BIU videos has my video recommendations littered with everything Korean. I'm tempted to start a K-drama, when Nim texts that he's outside.

I hustle out the door. He's leaning against a black tinted out SUV. His hands are deep in the pockets of his calf-length Nike puffer coat. I shrink down a little inside the Nike puffer the group sent me as a welcome present. I'm swallowed whole by so much fabric, but it's the perfect gift. The icy wind slaps across my eyes, watering my vision.

I smile at the tall Korean entertainer, and his eyes light up behind his mask.

I climb into the SUV, and he ducks in behind me and extends a hand.

"Nice to meet you Lorelei."

"Nice to meet you too."

When he lowers his mask, I lower mine too.

My throat tingles and I pull the mask back up.

"You'll get used to it."

He smiles a set of dimples and I light up again.

Hearing such good English from such an Asian guy is comforting.

Apart from the "Learn Korean In an Hour" video on the plane ride here, I can't speak a lick of his language. The only thing I can remember is how to read and write the word "teeth" and how to read and write the long e sound and the ah sound.

"The members can't wait to meet you."

"Seriously?"

"Seriously."

I can't respond to this since I remember the videos of the black women who traveled to South Korea. None of them felt beautiful living here. As much as I regret watching so many of their testimonies, I knew that I had to know what to expect here. Excitement for these guys to see me wasn't one of them.

"Your English is very good."

"Thank you, Lorelei that means a lot coming from you."

"You're welcome."

He stares at me for several seconds before his eyes get small again.

"What?"

He shakes his head and scratches the back of his gold hair.

"I'm kind of trying not to go full blown Korean on you and tell you, that you have big, beautiful, eyes. There it goes, I said it, now."

I can't help giggling.

"Thank you, Nim. And, uh, you are full blown Korean, so…"

"True. True. But I know better than to fanboy over your eyes like that."

"I don't mind."

"Tell me that after everybody you meet in South Korea stalks you over your eyes."

"At least they'll like something about me."

"Whatchewmean?"

"You do realize that I'm not full-blown Korean, right?"

"And?"

"And, I know what the beauty standards are here, and I'm never going to meet them."

He shakes his head again. The smile in his eyes long gone.

I want to ask him what he's thinking, but he's looking out the window. The SUV is parking in front of his home.

Nim says something to the driver and then shoulders the door. I step out and follow him to the front door that opens before we get to the top of the long flat steps.

All six band members are waiting, looking like live wallpaper. Nim has to shoo the guys back into the house so I can pass through. Korean phrases mumble on either side of me while I part the sea of guys.

Nim takes my coat away before I'm ready to let it go. I wish I could hide inside its long protection until it's time to leave.

I stand in the middle of their dining area, waiting for Nim to come back to rescue me. I dig my hands inside the pockets of my sailor striped Calvin Klein dress and stare down at my Chelsea boots. Anything to not have to look at them. They can't notice how ugly I am if I don't give them a chance to look at me.

The other tall guy in the group, Man-Seok forces me to interact with him. He starts a train of handshaking. Pop follows him, then Jung-ah, Tae-Woo, Jae-Hwa, and Ji. They're smiling, but that could mean anything.

Ji bows until Jae-Hwa smacks the back of his neck. He flips his head back up and catches his lavender hair before it falls back over his brow.

"Hi, nice to meet, I'm Ji."

I tell the group my name and they butcher it. I hear Rorylei, and Orelei, and every error in between. It sounds like Nim threatens them because they back away. He strides over to the fridge and pulls a mustard colored paper off. When he's back he tells me that lunch is in a few minutes. I look down at the shaking menu in his hand. I tell him to order for me and he and the guys laugh at my illiteracy.

"Don't worry, Lei. Please don't cry. We'll get some ramen some rice, and some other things to try." He raps.

I smile wide at him, forgetting to keep my head down. The guys repeat his rap and dance around me. Ji pulls my hand down when I cover my mouth to laugh. I clamp my lips shut and smile close-mouthed. Nim pulls me away to a seat at the tables they have smooshed together. Nim is the only person I feel comfortable enough with to face. I wish I still had my mask, so I would at least have somewhere to hide from all the eyes on me.

I start to relax when lunch arrives. The guys eat like starved animals, with little time to pay attention to my strange company. Nim offers me dishes I don't want, but I accept them anyway. "Korean 101," said that you accept what you're offered. Refusal often results in hurt feelings.

"We've got another few hours of rehearsal after coffee."

"Ok," I say nervously.

I know that I'm expected to have coffee with them, but I don't drink it.

"What's up?"

"Can I have tea?"

"Of course, you can have tea." Nim says something to Tae Woo, and he scampers off to the kitchen area.

He returns with a yellow box.

"Barley tea ok?"

I nod, afraid of what it tastes like.

The guys never stop what looks like teasing. They take turns waving at me. I don't know what else to do, so I wave back.

"Told you that they're excited to meet you," Nim whispers into my ear.

He bumps softly into me when I don't respond.

"I don't know what you've heard, but you're sexy as fuck, FYI."

He stands up and claps and the guys start clearing the table. He forbids me from helping which is good because I'm too stunned to move.

Ji brings my tea, and I bow and thank him. He smiles down at me, I can't remember if the bow is the right gesture to do in Korea, so he could be laughing at me. I tip my cup at him and sip the tea. It isn't the worst I've had, but I'd rather not have to drink another cup. I peek at the guys while they talk to each other. Their closeness is obvious from the way they touch and taunt each other. I look around for Nim, who's becoming my safety blanket. The way that the anxiety lessens whenever he's in my range of sight again, can't be healthy.

I can't breathe when Ji slides into the seat next to me, giggling for me to look at his phone screen. I welcome the distraction, happy that he doesn't want to talk. He shows me a video of Jae-Hwa looking like a puppy he's so young.

"Debut," Ji says, pointing and laughing at Jae-Hwa.

Jae-Hwa stands over Ji's shoulders leaning down and laughing at himself. His laughing makes me think it's ok to laugh too. He's a good sport about it all. Probably because he's so beautiful now. His strong, shapely thighs look good in the coated black denim he's wearing. I'd die if any of them get their hands on my debut performance. With the mischievous look in Ji's eyes, he's probably already working on it.

I stop laughing and give Jae-Hwa a thumbs up. He shakes his head.

"Bad. Very horrible."

I look at the screen again and try to see what he does. Aside from him looking like a newborn baby, his voice is as attractive as it is now.

"You sound good."

"Thank you."

I smile at Jae-Hwa. I can see why everybody goes out of their way to protect the maknae of the group. He's too cute to resist.

I thank Ji.

"You're welcome," Ji says in his funny way.

Nim takes me by the hand, and Ji pulls me back down.

Nim bugs his eyes at Ji, and Ji reluctantly releases me.

"Sorry about that. They're acting kind of weird right now, but they're just nervous."

I'm glad he can't see my eyes bulging while I follow him down the stairs. There's only one of me, if anyone is nervous it should be me.

"We never have guests at practice." He says before he does something in the stereo area.

I cock a brow at him.

"Millions of people watch your videos."

"Not the same."

The guys file downstairs a couple at a time. They get into formation and giggle while they stare at themselves in the mirrors. The second the music starts, they turn into something else. Nothing but masculine energy permeates from them. At the beginning of the song, everybody but Ji drops to their knees. When the violin score pierces the air, he spins inside the man-made circle like he's on ice skates. His two-block hair cut moves with his body. The shiny lavender layers whip around his brow and then settles back into place. Seeing him do this in person makes me more emotional than I want to be, sitting right in front of them. I can't take my eyes off of Ji, even though they are all blowing me away. I don't think I could perform like this in a million years, and this is just practice. I don't understand how Ji can have the command he does of so many dance styles. He executes the moves like he created them. He can't be further away from the original hip-hop scene, yet he does it better than any I've ever seen do it.

I'm scared when Nim waves me over after the song's over.

The guys are all teeth and sweat. I'm struggling to keep myself from going sasaeng over them.

"What do you think?"

"You guys are really good."

"Just good?"

I push his long arm and his dimples cave the sides of his cheeks in.

"Want to dance with us on the next one?"

"I'm good."

"Whatchewmean? George said you were going to teach us how it's done."

I could kill George and his big mouth. He has no right to challenge people this good on my behalf.

He looks at his members and they all step back, eager to obey the hierarchy of his elder status.

"I'm here to learn from you."

"We are the masters, but even the masters need refreshers."

He giggles with me but his eyes are dead serious.

"On the real, we want you to practice with us for our comeback performance."

"Where have you guys been?"

"Nowhere, we just like the way it sounds."

He gestures and Pop saunters over to the stereo to change the song.

I remember how much I liked this song yesterday on the plane. Or was it the day before yesterday? The 17-hour time difference makes it impossible to know what day it is in the US.

When they make space for me in their line-up, I realize that this is happening, whether I want it to or not.

The moves are easier to learn than I thought. They slow everything down for me, and I catch on quickly. When it's time to execute Ji's part, I know that I can't do it. Instead of embarrassing myself any more than I probably already have, I watch him instead.

Pop starts the song over and I sneak back to my seat. Watching from my chair is the best place for me. I'd love to learn how to dance like they do, but I'd rather practice on my own. They are too good to keep messing up in front of.

When the song ends, I catch Nim before he disappears upstairs.

"Thanks for allowing me to join you, but I'll sit the next ones out. I'll just slow you guys down."

He apologizes when he flings his hair and sweat lands on the bottom of my dress.

"George didn't tell you?"

"Tell me what?"

"You're performing with us." He winks and looks amused with himself before he disappears up the stairs.

When I turn back around giggles erupt from the dance studio. I try to play it off but I'm humiliated. George could've told me that I was coming here to work. Instead, he'd rather make me look like a fool to the biggest international band in the world. I should have known something was up when he took me shopping for new clothes. He never spends money on me, even though it's all mine.

George never tells me anything, which is why he is as good as fired. He pretended like this trip would be some kind of spiritual journey, but in reality, it's a payday for him-only.

I sulk back over to the chair as the pressure of what Nim just told me weighs on my chest. It's taking everything I have to sit in this seat without screaming. I hate George with everything inside of me.

A pair of black Jordan's stands in front of me and I look up. Ji's panting and looking down at me with a question in his eyes.

"Ok?" He gives me a thumbs up and I return the gesture.

I swipe at my temple and fan my angry burning face.

He walks back to a shelf and grabs a towel.

I take the thick peppermint scented towel.

"Thank you."

"You're welcome."

He takes a seat on the floor and hugs his knees to his chest. He says a string of gibberish and I temporarily forget to feel sorry for myself. The guys are teasing him about the way he dances, over exaggerating his moves. Their imitations crack him up until his head tips back and he's hollering. His crooked front tooth is visible from this position. Despite this barely noticeable flaw, his smile still looks perfectly straight. To see him smile any other time is to never know it's there. He is unwilling to fix it after five years in the industry. He makes me feel better about my appearance. I've got the same pedestrian-straight smile I've had since the day my last baby tooth grew in. There's pressure from George to update my smile as he calls it, but he won't pay for it.

Ji falls back until he bumps into my shin. He springs up like he broke my leg.

"Sorry. Sorry." He lifts one hand while he says this and I tell him it's ok. He's only 5'9" but he feels strong as an ox. His heaviness against my leg felt good. So good that I wish his friends would make him fall against me some more.

We practice for six hours. The whole time my body is like an antenna. I can feel Ji's energy dancing around me, even if I can't always see him. This must be what a shark feels like when he smells blood. He can concentrate on nothing except getting to that lovely scent, and having a bite of it.

When practice is over, I'm anxious to go back to my temporary home, but my body's too sore to move very fast. Nim doesn't look like he plans on going anywhere when I ask him to call the SUV back. He's pulling the sheets off his bed, and changing them, while I wait in the hallway for him to give me the number. Two sheets and a comforter fly out the door. Minutes later he scoops up the linen and tells me good night.

I swallow my words when I remember my Korean manners. I want to grill him about how I'm going to stay here with none of the things that I need, but I know I won't succeed.

I stop Nim at the door to his room when he attempts to pass by.

"Thanks, Nim, but I need my things at my apartment. Wouldn't it be better if I went back there tonight?"

"We have everything you need here. Have you seen how much makeup we have to wear?"

I hate that he's so funny while I'm trying to get out of this.

"We keep plenty of toothbrushes around here so you should be good."

I recall the damp toothbrush sitting in a zip-lock bag in my purse. All eight of us sat as a group brushing our teeth after lunch. In Korea, brushing after every meal is as commonplace, and communal as eating every meal together.

"And what am I supposed to wear after I get out of the shower?" The guys laugh around me, and my stomach twists again. I can't tell how much English they know, but their timing is too good for the laughing to be a coincidence.

He speaks Korean over my head. The laughing stops, but I can feel the eyes behind me.

"Don't worry, we'll figure something out. But you stay here as our guest. You've worked hard. I would be a poor host if I didn't provide you rest."

I can see someone approaching through the frosted pane before he knocks on the door.

I'm sitting at the seat at Nim's desk facing the door when I tell the person to come in.

Ji holds a pile of clothes between his hands and holds them out for me. He looks down at the floor like I'm naked.

"Thanks."

"You're welcome. Clothes fit you best."

He's probably right since he's the shortest, but I still don't want to wear them. I've soaked through my thong, so I'll have to go commando.

"You're welcome. My clothes fit best." I say.

I repeat myself until he's mimicking me. When he struggles on the L sound I slow down. When the L sound still stumps him, I pinch the tip of my tongue with my fingertips and say the L sound again. He does it too and smiles at how much easier it is to do it this way. I push his hand away the next few times so he doesn't grow dependent on the tongue grab, but he dodges my next swats. He licks the spit from his lips when the mini English lesson is over.

He pinches his tongue and asks me, "Will you teach English?"

It's hard to say no to him up this close.

"Maybe."

He smiles.

I didn't say yes, but he doesn't seem to care. As long as I didn't say no, he knows he's won. He wishes me goodnight and leaves, closing the door softly behind him.

I smell his clothes and the familiar fabric softener teleports me back to the Midwest. Hollywood will never be my home, even if I live out the rest of my life there. I sniff too hard and activate my sensitive nose again. I race to my purse and chew on a tongue-numbing allergy pill so it'll work faster. I unfold the gray Puma hoodie, red Puma short sleeve, and gray Puma skinny joggers.

I check Nim's personal bathroom for cameras but it's no use. I'll never find it if he's any good at surveillance. Checking for cameras before I undress is a paranoid habit I learned from George. As long as I live, I'll never be able to undress without his voice in my head. The stall doesn't look used, it's so spotless. The tiling is China blue with several bottles of soap that all smell like desert. There's a ledge inside that I'm tempted to sit on until I imagine how many other things have happened on this ledge.

I feel naked in spite of the too big clothes I have on. I feel bad for leaving remnants of myself behind in his clothes. It doesn't help that I can't stop thinking about him. The thoughts make me produce more of what I'm trying my best not to do.

At some point, I sneeze myself awake. I sneeze like I sniffed a line of coarse black pepper in my dream. A knock at Nim's door makes me hop out of his bed. The cold floor tempts me to curse but I can't stop sneezing long enough to get a complaint out.

Ji's standing on the other side of the door. His biceps pop when he hands me a bottle of allergy pills. I try not to stare at him

13

in his sleeveless shirt, but it's hard not to. I try to sneeze quieter when the next attack starts. I try to tell him I have my own, but he points at his bottle with a thumb up, and I sense it's the real deal. Not the cheap dollar store shit George always buys.

"Two." He says uncapping the bottle.

He taps two pills smaller than the ones I've been taking, but I take them, desperate to not wake anyone else up. He pushes the bottle into my bosom, and I accept them.

"Thanks," I say when my nose gives me a break.

"You're welcome."

He smiles when he successfully pronounces the L sound with his new trick.

I can see Jae-Hwa giving him shit right now for doing that.

"Did I wake you up?"

He whisks his hair away and shakes his head. His dark roots show underneath the pastel lavender.

I wonder what's keeping him up at 3 am, but I can't keep my eyes open for too long because the tiny pills are already working.

January 3

A battalion of alarms wakes me up. I know it's early because the light coming in from outside through the blinds is still dull. All my muscles and bones hurt. If today's anything like yesterday, there's nothing but sweat waiting for me.

I accept the sweet potatoes Nam ladles into my shallow bowl. I never even notice sweet potatoes in the grocery store until Thanksgiving. Even then, I never eat them. I smile at jokes as if I understand them. I don't care about any of that. My only goal is to survive this month. I turn my phone off when George texts me to call. I'm too nervous to talk to him, even though he's the one who should be scared.

The guys are going shopping and then to lunch, according to Nim. I beg him to let me stop at my apartment first. He agrees and apologizes for making me uncomfortable.

The air quality is better today so no masks. I think I'll actually get a chance to enjoy a sneeze free day until Nim texts me to come back outside. I peek out the blinds of my apartment and the van's still there. Waiting for me.

I pretend to not like shopping very much so they don't notice that I'm broke. I sit on the expensive chairs in the Gucci store and stare at my blank phone screen. I've always wondered what it was like in here. It's as luxurious as I imagined it would be. This trip would be even better if I could join in the fashion show the guys are putting on for me.

Ji exits his dressing room waving a black blouse with small, but succulent red lips kissing all over it. I nod and smile at him. It looks just like something he would wear. It's exactly the kind of shirt I would've picked, but somehow, he'll manage to make it look even better. The choices the guys make show me that they style themselves, nowadays anyway. Whoever taught them did a great job. They know exactly how to push the envelope without going overboard.

I'm relieved when Nim says that we're on our way back to my apartment until he says that I should bring all of my things with me. I close my eyes while he says this, knowing that it is pointless to argue my side of the story. It makes perfect sense for me to already be there every day to practice. If I'm expected to perform with them at the end of the month, I need every waking moment to learn what they make look easy.

I practice Ji's signature dance in Nim's room until someone knocks on the door for practice. I spin another few times until I remember that whoever is on the other side can see my figure as well as I can see theirs.

"Ok, thanks. Be right there." I say diving in Nim's bed.

I peek over the bed and the figure's still there.

I step out the bed and open it, ready to hustle down to the basement. Ji stops me.

He hands me a bottle of water and a hand towel.

"Thank you."

He motions like he's sneezing. It looks like a question.

I pull out my phone from the waistband of my leggings and type into my translator.

[Thank you so much. Your pills worked like a miracle.]

He takes my phone and types into it.

[You're welcome. I'll make sure you always have them. All you have to do is ask.]

My eyes water, but I smile through it.

"Thank you."

He motions me in front of him, and I quickly walk down to the basement.

Nim positions me into my spot in the dance line. Before he starts the music, he explains that I'm to mirror all of Ji's parts. In some songs, I'm to be the personification of his passion. I don't fully follow him until I start acting out the part. For the majority of the song, I'm dancing in tandem with the whole group. Right before the beat drops to the climax, I'm to push Ji down with one hand. He falls back next to me, and I take his spot. My role seems to be someone he can direct his passions. It isn't until we're dancing that I see how genius the idea is. I've never seen anything like it in a performance.

I channel every bit of talent that I used to have into this performance. It's only practice but the guys dance like their lives depend on it. When the song is over the guys look at me shocked. I'm nothing like the woman they met yesterday. Before I was afraid and dressed all wrong for the flexibility I need to dance well. Now I can move my entire body without fear of ripping my tights and scuffing my brand-new suede booties. I feel free. It takes me a few minutes to snap out of my head while we catch our breath.

Nim looks like he doesn't know what to say while he makes his way over to me.

"Lei, you did not just do that."

"Do what?" I pant.

"The damn thang."

I laugh at his dated slang.

"Thanks."

"No, thank you."

I'm glad he's relieved that I'm not the disappointment I must have seemed like yesterday. I'm still struggling with Ji's move, but I'm slowly starting to remember that I've got talent too.

Nim says that they practice every day for twelve hours. A few days ago, I would've choked on my water, but it doesn't surprise me. There's no way you can get as good as they are with an hour a day. I don't ask how much time they spend in the studio for fear he'll say they spend the other twelve hours there.

There are so many courses for lunch. Today, I understand why. I wolf down two containers of spicy chicken ramen, sweet and sour pork, and a bowl of rice and vegetables. Twelve full hours of sweat will burn all of these calories. It's such an efficient way of staying in shape that I'm considering keeping this kind of schedule in LA. Maybe then, after George sees me working so hard, he'll see that I deserve access to my own money. My appetite takes a nose dive. I place my chopsticks on the napkin next to my bowl of rice and veggies. I want to roll my leggings down so that my food baby can breathe, but I'm not that comfortable yet.

After tea and coffee, Ji leads us in stretch. This is the first thing that I'm actually in the mood to do. He plays a slow jam while he leads the stretch. When I notice everybody ignoring Ji, I close my eyes. I try to ignore the new rubber smell of my pink mat and relax. I breathe in through my nose and out through my nose.

I lay down, put my legs together and stretch. My hands are clasped and pulling in the opposite direction. I slowly lift my legs, up and over my head. When my toes touch the floor, I snap my eyes open. The room is quiet when I slowly make my way back to a flat position. Everyone is staring.

"Show us?" Ji asks.

I look around and the guys are all nodding.

"Show us again." Tae Woo says.

"Yeah, do, again." Man-Seok urges.

I roll up to my knees and pair the guys up. They push their partner's legs over their heads.

"Oh, my gawd. I can't. You show." Pop whines.

I pinch his shoulder.

"No."

They all pout.

Ji's on my mat waiting for me when I come back.

"Show me?"

I straighten his legs and help him to pull them up over his head.

"See? Can't do it. You show."

When I refuse, he calls Nim.

Nim comes out and he asks me to show him my move.

He smirks.

I show the move quickly, but there's no way to avoid giving everyone seconds.

"Excellent. Lei, you lead stretch from now on." He kneads the back of his neck.

Ji pokes his tongue out and I want to strangle him.

"Great going," Ji says.

I roll my eyes.

He doesn't understand my attitude. He springs up to his feet and mimics his dance routine from earlier.

"Oh, thank you." My cheeks burn. I've wanted his approval so badly that I'm embarrassed that I'm too busy pouting to enjoy it.

Nim calls us over to a table. Everyone else is already there when Ji and I take a seat at the large rectangular table.

We sit, and the guys take turns winking at me on the sly. They're so funny the way they all work in sync to tease each other and flirt with me. The longer I'm around them the more I'm beginning to think that some of the flirting may be real. I remind myself that these are guys at the end of the day. They are way too hip to only be into Asian girls. They are international playboys. There's no way that they turn down the beautiful women throwing themselves at them.

My mom used to say that everybody's black in the dark. She also used to say that all pussy is pink. I close my eyes at the cringey memory.

Nim barrels ahead with 100 mph Korean. I couldn't keep up even if I did speak the language. He's getting down to business judging by the somber faces staring back at him. Ji keeps answering texts and I'm scared for him because Nim looks like he doesn't play.

Nim, Pop, and Jung Ah are the rappers of the group. With Nim being the lead rapper. They have all the swag of any wannabe gangster in America. It's like they took Ice Cube and dunked him into a vat until he came out looking like Nim. These guys are so good that I was in love with their rap before I knew what they were talking about. After translation, my respect for their talents only grew deeper.

Ji, Jung-Ah, and Jae-Hwa are the dancers of the group. They put most entertainers to shame. These three have energy that comes from some unknown place. None of them dance alike, they couldn't if they tried to. For instance, Jung-Ah is a natural dancer. He moves with sharp precision that makes every move he does seem super easy. Jae-Hwa being the maknae of the group, is usually front and center. His dance style is very attractive and skilled. He's got a baby face, with a man's body. The combo makes it hard to decide whether what he does on stage is cute or sexy. The twenty-two-year-old could be the sexiest man in the group. If Ji didn't exist. Ji is indescribable. To put words to what he does on stage is hard. He is je ne sais quoi, grace, power, and sexiness all rolled into one. He can go from cute to daddy in seconds. He is what sex would look like if it was a person. And that's just the dancing. They all sing like angels. Tae-Woo is an Asian Barry White with his sexy unusually deep voice. He's twenty-three and part of the maknae line, right in the middle of Jaw-Hwa and Ji. Jae-Hwa is a lead singer along with Ji. Ji sings like it's his last performance. He's often crying more than the girls listening to him. Ji raps too, but he's so good at it that Nim admits that if he puts him on more songs, he fears he'll be out of a job.

Man-Seok is the eldest of the group and a heartthrob. He's over six-foot-tall, and all the guys envy him for it. Even Nim who stands eye to eye with him admires his model good looks. Man-Seok's thick shapely lips make it easy for him to make the fandom to go nuts. As long as he's there for them to scream at, they don't care what he does. He's got an attractive voice that surprises me every time I hear him sing. To say that Man-Seok's dancing isn't strong is unfair because comparing him to the dance line is unfair. His height makes his moves look different in a way that looks like he doesn't have to try as hard to look cool. The shorter guys envy him for it.

If I had to take a guess, Pop is the one most likely to date a black woman. I've not researched it as much as I want to, but he came from a tough background. He seems cold and unapproachable, but he's one of the most thoughtful members of the group. His raps always make me look at him with more respect after I've translated what the hell, he sounds so angry about. I definitely feel his pain over having to choose eating or catching a bus home to a place that was too far away to walk to. I have to make life decisions over trivial shit all the time. He's a closet dancer and is very good at it. During practice, he seems to pull back the better he dances. I don't understand it, but I suspect that his mysteriousness is what makes the girls go sasaeng over him.

Ji finally puts his phone down and I can breathe again. Nim looks pissed, and my presence is the only thing saving him from getting cursed out. That reminds me to ask Ji to teach me how to curse in Korean.

When I was in high school, I had no patience for the foreign language classes I had to take. Instead of paying attention to the teacher, I was looking up curse words on the internet. When I saw how impressed people were that I could insult them, that was all I cared to learn.

Ji taps his fingers on his phone screen. I can't help looking. It doesn't dawn on me that I'm reading English until I'm halfway down the screen.

I race to Nim after he calls Ji up to talk after the meeting. He calls Ji up in Korean, but I can tell by his vibe that he's about to go off. At least I know that if Ji refuses to teach me profanity, that Nim would be a good teacher.

"Can I talk to you for a sec?" I can tell that he hates that his manners won't allow him to make me wait, so he turns his back to Ji and bends down to hear me.

"Forgive me if I'm jumping to conclusions, but don't be mad at Ji for texting during the meeting."

"And why shouldn't I be mad at such disrespect?"

"Because he was translating for me."

Nim looks back at Ji and then looks at me. He covers his face with both hands and dips his head back, sucking in the air behind his fingers.

"Dang, Lei, I'm so sorry. I forgot all about translating for you."

"It's ok."

"No, it's not. I'm a horrible host, forgive me." He dips his head and immediately exits the room. He seems hurt and I can't help but feel bad for being the reason for it.

We finish practice and the members disappear.

Ji hands me his phone. He's written many things on it. I speed read to take it all in. It says that he gave up his room for me so that Nim can have his room back. He says the leader deserves the privacy for having so many burdens to bear.

I don't want anyone to give up anything, so I type it, but his mind goes unchanged. His honor is more important than sleeping in his bed for a month.

Ji doesn't have to type it for me to see that he took a great risk for me today. He was willing to look like a bad apple in front of his whole group for me.

I want to thank him, but it doesn't feel like enough. Instead, I type that we can start his English lesson tonight. This lightens his mood and it's as if nothing ever happened. When I take his phone back and type in my request he cracks up. His body folds up until he's rolling around on the floor clutching his stomach. I don't know if that's a yes or a no, but whatever it is, I'm happy I could make him smile again.

Preparing for Ji to come into his own room is nerve-wracking. The fact that he's going to have to look at my mouth makes me exfoliate my lips until they're raw. I wish I could do that sample teeth whitening kit George gave me a while ago. My teeth aren't too bad, but like everything else lately, I don't feel like I measure up. Every member of the group looks like they were born with perfect white teeth. There's nothing artificial looking about their smiles. None of them have huge ill-fitted teeth. I give up after the fourth slathering of cocoa tinted Carmex on my lips. I'm thinking too much about this. Why am I changing my shirt again? My Pink stretch pants are cuter with a halter top, but that outfit begs him to make me scream the curses I want to learn. He knocks on the door to his own room, and I tell him he has permission to come in.

He's dressed in a white tee, tapered hunter green polo joggers, and gray Puma slips. His thick black rimmed nerd glasses make it hard to think straight. His lavender hair is swept back and I want to run my hand over the glossy mound. I sit in one of the recliners furthest away from the bed. I haven't so much as touched it. He showed me the bed dressing still in the package before he changed his bed. He even purchased a powder pink duvet to make me feel more comfortable.

He types into his phone and hands it to me.

When I don't respond he takes it off my lap.

[Don't be scared.] He hands the phone back.

[I'm not scared.]

He saunters over to the bed, kicks his Puma slips off and waits for me.

I swallow down the sour taste in my mouth and sit Indian Style on the edge of the bed.

I don't have time to react when he scoops me closer to him.

"Don't fall."

He's smiling, and I'm trying not to make it obvious that I was sniffing him. He smells like nothing. No body odor or strong cologne, he just smells like man. There's a faint smell of something spiced in his hair product but it's barely detectable. I want to lean over and sniff more, even though nothing will be there. I'm just as intrigued as if there was.

He waves a hand in front of my eyes.

"Sorry."

His eyes smile until they disappear. I look down at his phone.

He's still staring at me when I can face him again. He's waiting for me to start.

[What's so funny?]

He pulls his phone away from me and smiles while he types.

[I hate how well my members know me.]

I read the line four times, and I still can't decode his message.

I roll my hands toward him so he'll explain, but he shakes his head, He removes his glasses to swipe his neat hair. He brings a thick piece of it back with him when he's done messing it up. The piece dances on the tips of his eyelashes and I am starting to regret agreeing to this.

[They could see that you are a natural beauty. I thought that it was makeup and effects.]

[Do you agree with them?]

"I do." He says.

His unexpected English takes me by surprise every time. When I look over at him, he's taking his entire lower lip into his mouth.

I return his phone to him.

He steals my phone when I pull it out from my waistband and texts himself.

I lean back on my hands and think about what we could talk about. I've always wanted to be a teacher, but now that I have the perfect chance, I'm drawing a blank. I don't see the need for teaching him words and phrases he'll never use. I click my phone off and start as natural a conversation as I can.

"Hi, Ji."

His eyes light up when he recognizes my phrase and greets me back.

"Did you have a good day today?"

I can see the wheels spinning in his head. He caught some words, but I'm not making sense.

"Good day?"

"Oh, yes. Good day."

I hop off the bed.

"We danced hard, today didn't we?"

I point between us do a body roll, and inflect my voice until he's repeating my sentence. He doesn't quite get it, so I type it, allow him to read it once, and then, erase it.

He waves a hand through his hair until he's rubbing his neck. "Yes."

The fatigue in his response reminds me of how exhausted I am too.

I type for him to pay more attention to my body language. That since we're dancers, we speak using our bodies more than the average person.

He types back that he thinks it's intelligent that I've thought of that.

He slips his glasses back on and swings his legs off the bed.

I stop him.

His arm is tight and hard when I attempt to pull him back to face me.

He drops his head, defeated.

He scolds me with his eyes but he can't change my mind.

I stare at the sharp angle of his jaw until he swings back on the bed. He reluctantly opens his mouth and quietly teaches me my first Korean curse word. I have to concentrate on his lips more intensely since he's barely saying it loud enough for me to hear.

I stare at his dark lips and realize how much I like full lips on a man. I never have before, but his lips are a different story.

"Why?" He says after I repeat his curse.

The perfect English precision of his question makes me tingle.

[Such filth shouldn't come out of your mouth.]" He types.

He speaks into his translator app, and I speak the word into mine.

My translation engine is spitting out nothing but gibberish.

He takes my hand, still wrapped around my phone, and brings hit close to his lips. He repeats the word slowly.

I look down at the results and smile. I catch my tongue between my teeth I'm so excited to know a Korean curse word.

Now that I know it, it's only right that I teach it to him. So, I repeat fuck, until he rushes out of his room.

January 4

I love it when it rains. The threat of rain in the air is one of my favorite scents. I miss it most about the Midwest. But this isn't the sound of rain because I'm not there. I'm a world away and this is the sound and smell of water coming from the shower.

Ji waves at me when he exits the bathroom. I reach for the hoodie he gave me and race into my slips. I escape out of the room and sneak into the living room. His comforter sits folded in one corner of the couch.

"Sorry."

He joins me on his new bed.

It's hard to stop seeing the image of him wrapped from the waist down in a navy towel.

He slides closer to me and shares his phone screen.

[I thought I could slip in and slip out.]

I read quickly, while I stab at the crust in the corners of my eyes on the sly.

He laughs quietly.

[When I saw you were up,]

I watch him type.

[I played a game with you. I won.] He snickers.

I can't face him now. I look like shit, and he looks like he's ready to keep winning.

I try to process his texts, occasional English, and wit. The language barrier makes it hard for me to catch how intelligent and funny he is.

"Sorry." He says again.

I want to say it's ok, but my teeth feel like velvet.

[Why don't I switch with you? I can sleep on the couch. Or I can go back to my studio apartment.]"

[I'll use another shower from now on.]

[No.]

[Yes.]

[No.]

I try to get up, but he pulls on the waist of my leggings until I'm sitting back down.

[I need to brush my teeth if you haven't already noticed.]

He faints, and I try to get back up.

He catches me, laughing against my back.

[If you were my girl, I'd kiss you, mb and all.]

I giggle at his schoolboy message.

["Have you ever even had a girlfriend?] I joke.

He shakes his head, purses his lips.

"Nope."

He's serious.

He's definitely not a virgin, but I was wrong about him having a girlfriend.

[So, you've never liked a girl enough to ask her to be your girlfriend?]

It's a long time before he types.

[I've had one-sided love.]

[Did you tell her how you felt?]

He shakes his head.

"Duh."

He's confused so I type.

[Duh!]

His eyes smile.

[Why don't you tell her now?]

[That has long since passed.]

[I'd bet she loves you now.]

[What makes you think that?]

I crinkle my brows.

[I don't know, the fact that you're in BIU and you're the sexiest dancer I've ever seen.]

He's watching me type, so I can't erase the text.

"Thank you."

I nod.

[Are you ready to work hard in the studio today?]

"Yes."

[Sure?]

I bug my eyes at him, and he takes the phone back.

[Good because you're not good enough yet.]

My heart twists.

[Yes, I am.]

[Not yet, but you'll have to get there or our reputation will be ruined.]

This time he doesn't stop me from leaving when I get up.

I plan on staying away from Ji during practice, but Nim and the guys leave for the day. I don't want to disappoint Nim by wasting the day fuming in Ji's room, but I can't help it. Ji has no right to tell me, a star in my own right that I'm not good enough. I dance circles around everybody that dares to step on the stage with me. Facts. I don't do all that synchronized shit BIU does, I dance from raw talent, can he say that? Could he do all that fucking twirling if someone hadn't taught him how to do it?

I take the steps two at a time to the basement. Ji's standing with his hands clasped behind his back like he's been waiting for me the whole time. I meet him in the middle of the floor, hands strangling my waist ready to dance. He may be the shortest guy, but his height still towers over my 5'1" frame.

He takes a stride back and does at least three spins before ending with his hands snaked over his head.

I can't do the shit and he knows it. He lowers his hands and slows the move down for me until it's in four parts. The three spins and the transition into the arms snaked over my head. I attempt the first spin and before I can get halfway around, he slaps my knee down.

"Again."

I look at him like he's lost his mind.

He grasps my knee between his fingertips as soon as I lift my leg. He pushes hard enough for me to teeter.

"Strong."

I get what he's saying but he has one more time to touch me before I smack him back.

I attempt the spin again, and he smacks my knee back down.

His smacks are painless, but he's pissing me off.

I cross my arms, out of breath.

He steps in front of me and snaps his fingers in front of my nose.

"Use this. Anger. Strong, spin."

He spins in front of me so hard that his body feels like a propeller.

I don't move, because I know I'll do it wrong. Furthermore, his words from earlier are ringing true and I can't stand it. It's like I left all my talent in America.

I run for the stairs, knowing that I'm being a weak little bitch, but I can't let him see me cry.

I almost call George, but I can't find my phone.

Ji helps himself into his room again.

His arrogance makes me want to puke.

"Lorelei."

I can tell he's holding his tongue, but that cutesy bullshit won't work. I'm starting to see why his love was one-sided. He probably told her she wasn't good enough to be his girlfriend yet, but that she would have to be by the end of the school year.

Siri's male voice cuts into the angry silence.

[You're not letting go when you dance. That's why you're not good enough yet. The talent is there, but you're holding back. When you're on that stage that's the one time where you can be as sad or as angry or as sexy as you're feeling. Whcn you hold that back you're not showing your talent, you're hiding it.]

I snatch his phone.

[But there's a way to help me get the steps perfected, and your method isn't it.]

[You can take it.]

This little bast...

[This business is not for pussies, even if you happen to have one. And if you want to learn how to say that, I can tell you right now.]

I accidentally laugh at Siri before I tear up again.

Ji doesn't give a fuck and it hurts, but I obviously need it, so I follow him back downstairs.

No matter how many times I try, he smacks my knee down. I can't execute the move with whatever anger he wants.

When we take a break, Ji gives me his phone. I don't want to touch anything of his, but I read it anyway.

[I need to give you something.]

He leaves his phone with me while he jogs into the sound studio.

I look up at him.

He raises his mean eyebrows for me to take the bag.

I push the Gucci logo tissue paper aside and peek inside.

He gives up and drops to his knees and unburdens the bag. He holds the black shirt with lipstick kisses out for me.

I won't touch it.

He sits back down folds the shirt in his lap and takes his phone.

[Don't you like it?]

[No.] I lie.

[I want you to have it.]

[I don't want it.]

He blows out an angry breath and stuffs the beautiful shirt back inside the bag.

[Will you let me feed you, or are you on hunger strike too?]

By the time we get back from an awkwardly silent dinner, everybody else is back. I'm mad at Nim for leaving me alone with him. The guys are happy to see Ji again, and he them, so I take the opportunity to go straight to bed.

January 5

My nostrils hate me in the morning. I'm tempted to take all the little white pills Ji gave me. Anything to keep my nose from the constant assault. Ji's allergies are flared up too, but I don't care. I feel bad that he blesses me after every sneeze.

My plan to stick to Jung-Ah all day is a good one. He allows me to make all the mistakes I want and he never makes me feel like the dirt on the bottom of his shoe.

When it's time for Ji's solos, the guys look at him like they wish they could be him. He must be the angriest person in the world because he does not miss a step. I would never believe that he's one of the clumsiest members in the group if I had not seen him fall in so many videos.

I can't see how I'll be able to pull this performance off. I could be ready in three or four months, but not by the end of this one. Why the hell would they agree to let me perform with them? George's reach can't be that long that he can sway the better judgment of the best group in South Korea.

I know I can't ignore George forever, so I finally take his call. He talks at me, while I count down from one hundred. My head throbs while I struggle to keep my mouth shut. Any illusion of what I thought an entertainer was, is over. Working myself to nubs for strangers to applaud me, feels like slavery. None of this is worth it. I want to curse until my throat breaks. This wannabe, Don King won't let me breathe without him knowing about it first. At this point being a normal person would

"I'm not even going to ask you why you haven't called, because I know there's a good reason for it."

I don't answer.

"Is there a good reason why I haven't heard from you?"

He sounds like a mom if said mom had a bald head, a Mr. T goatee, and the fashion sense of Goldie the Mack.

"Why didn't you tell me I was coming out here to perform?"

"Because you wouldn't have gone, now what's kept you from calling? And don't tell me you've been too busy because I speak to their manager every day."

"What's my cut?"

"Your cut?"

"You know, my compensation for exposing me to lung cancer."

"You are so dramatic. Look, Lorie. I told you that when you're new to the business that you can't expect to make it rain right away. I told you I would take care of you."

"If I'm not getting paid, we can't keep working together."

"Not funny."

"Did you hear me laughing? The next time I see you, you'd better have my fucking money."

I hang up, but there's little relief in tapping the red circle.

The guys are all still milling around the studio even though practice is over. Some of them are dancing, and some are admiring their reflections in the floor to ceiling mirrors. I find a spot, large enough to spin in. I repeat the last line I told George in my head over and over again. I'm so pissed that he made me go there with him, that when Ji yells "Aaah, Lei!" from across the studio, I notice what I'm doing. I look at my reflection and my arms snake over my head. I've never completed the triple spin until now. Ji's the first one to reach me even though he's the furthest away. He embraces me with my arms still up in the air. He's saying something in Korenglish. All I can catch is cruelty before the other members smother me with hugs. Nim decides that it's time for me to become a proper Korean and pop bottles.

I don't drink much, and I'm glad that I don't have to. Faking the funk is better than impoliteness in Korea. I want to know what Ji said before the other members bum rushed me but I'm still mad at him.

[Are you still my English tutor, or should I find another?]

I glance down at the furthest table from mine. Ji's staring at me, unblinking.

"Good day?" Ji asks as soon as he closes his bedroom door behind him.

It's hard to know how much English Ji actually knows. His understanding is so fragmented that he's constantly throwing me off. But then, I'll say the simplest phrase and nothing registers.

I don't have the energy to lie, so I shake my head.

"Why?"

"I had a bad phone call with my manager."

He looks like he understands that I had a bad phone call. I have to type the word manager for him.

[What's troubling you?]

[He doesn't communicate with me. He makes decisions like my opinion doesn't matter. You do remember that you have my phone number, don't you?]

[I like this way better.]

I don't want to like what he's typing to me. I'm too mad to admit that I like sharing his phone too.

"Sorry for your call." He says catching himself from taking the phone to type words he already knows.

His smile chips away at my attitude.

[The house is so quiet at night.]

His top lip curls.

[Everyone is on their very best behavior for you. You should hear them. All they talk about is whether Lorelei would like this to eat. What we should do to make you more comfortable, or what they should wear, and if you would like it. It's sickening.]

He rolls his eyes

His words are working and I hate it.

I enjoy watching him squirm when I ask him to continue his lesson on Korean Curse. He reluctantly recites a handful of my favorites into my translator so he doesn't have to repeat them.

The handful he shares with me tonight should make me fluent in Korean curse, which is a victory for me.

[What's your boyfriend's name?]

[No boyfriend.]

[How is that possible?]

[The same way it's possible that you've never had a girlfriend.]

He squints one eye.

[What was your last boyfriend like?]

[No comment.]

[Did you like the shirt?]

The fucking shirt again.

[What does it matter?]

[Because I want it to please you.]

He scoots closer when I scoot back.

[What were you saying earlier?]

He stares at his phone for a long time after I give it back.

[I said that I'm sorry and that I didn't mean the cruelty. My teacher taught me hard at first. It worked, but it was hard to hear the truth about what kind of performer I was at that point.]

He texts more.

[You are an excellent dancer Lorelei, but you rest on your natural abilities too much. I knew you were doing that because I used to be the same person. Nobody could touch me, so I was unteachable. My teacher had to break me of that attitude before I could become better.]

This was not what I wanted this conversation to turn into. It's hard to keep hearing and reading that I'm not good enough.

[It wasn't until I saw you picking up the steps so effortlessly that I could see why my teacher was so harsh with me. I never would've kept going all those times I wanted to quit if I hadn't had his training.]

I look at him and his glossy eyes are hard to keep staring at. I beg him inside my head not to cry, but a tear falls anyway. I touch his face. He touches mine. I don't realize I'm crying too until his fingers keep wiping tears away. His hand wraps around the nape of my neck and I can't resist him.

His feather-soft lips chisel away at me until my body slips underneath his. I hope he can't tell how much I need him. That I can't let go of his body. He's slipping our pants down, but can he tell that this is more than me getting one off? He fills my body to the brim with his. He feels better than I imagined he would. His arms wrapped around me, are my protection, if only for a little while. His strong, and deep grind into me is for my pleasure, even if it has to end. The Korean he whispers into my ear is saying that it is only me, it always was me, even if it's impossible for it to be true. I'm not a whore right now, I am his love. The woman he's always desired, right in the palms of his hands. This isn't the best orgasm I've ever had, while my muscles contract him in and out of me in slow motion. I'm not crying because the throbbing won't go faster, instead of slowly trying to kill me. He bursts inside of me, and his warmth makes me feel beautiful. He sways his hips side to side to get every last drop of me. We nip each other's lips to keep quiet. I shush his apology for letting go inside of me. He doesn't seem to care when I tell him that birth control is written into my contract. He seems disappointed that he couldn't keep going. He rolls us up in the comforter and stays a while. I understand when he has to go. No matter how long it would have lasted it was always going to end.

January 6

I can't see anything but Ji. Even when his members are dead in the center of my gaze, my vision still searches for him.

The only thing keeping me from unraveling like yarn is practice. Not only am I expected to learn Ji's harder than hell dance numbers, but I've got to learn his parts of the songs. Thankfully, I haven't lost my singing ability. I easily impress the group when I hit the studio.

No one knows that we got down last night. As happy as I am for his discretion, I wish that he would show me something. Just a tiny fissure that he's as fucked up as I am, but he's giving nothing away.

Nim congratulates himself that he was right that the studio would be a cakewalk for me. That was until he told me that they're known for never lip singing. These guys don't waver while they dance which is unheard of in the US. So many singers in the states lip sing that it'd be easier to name the people that don't do it. I don't, but I also ease the dancing up so that I can sing well.

Nim assigns Ji to me for the rest of the day to rehearse in masks so I can get used to the air restriction. I hope that spending so much time together won't make him want to stop coming at night for his English lesson.

"I'm sorry." Ji says.

"For what?"

He types into his phone.

[For making you avoid me all day.]

[I thought you were avoiding me.]

He closes in on me like he's seconds away from kissing me.

[I didn't want to leave or wash you off.]

[I wanted you to stay too. But you did wash, right? Lol.]

He smirks and I don't know if that's a yes or no. I don't care.

Ji types, [Will you do something for me?]

[Anything.]

[Forget about your previous bf?]

[You're the only one bringing him up.]

He flexes his jaw and smirks.

I take a mental snap of his face and note how good his slightly more slanted left eye looks. I've never seen a person wear flaws so well. I hold my breath and type.

[Will you do something for me?]

He's staring down at me but I can't look up.

[Will you never forget me?]

His arms are wrapping around my middle until Nim raps his way down the stairs.

Nim talks us in half and half. I try to concentrate. Ji listens to Nim but keeps his eyes on me the whole time.

"Anyways, we're going out for dinner. If you guys want to keep practicing, I'll let the Uber know."

Ji deuces Nim.

"Cool, see you later." He deuces us and takes quick strides back upstairs.

We practice until everyone's gone. He showers in Jae-Hwa's room and I shower in his. I try to cry it out in his shower, but I'm still tearing up when he's back in his room again.

Ji kisses underneath my lower lids. His soft kisses make me cry more.

I comb my fingers through the roots of his thick hair and drop my head. It feels like my nervous system is waking up after a lifetime of hibernation. All the synapses are firing at the same time.

He takes my phone and hurls it on his bed when I try to slip it out my back pocket. He hands me his phone and then hugs me again.

I clutch my arms around his neck while I try to type. The way he fusses over sharing his phone makes me weaker every time he does it.

[I'm sorry for being such a bad student. I hope I'm getting better.]

I hand him the phone over my shoulder. When he squeezes me tighter, I know he's finished reading. He tosses his phone on the bed too, and I wrap my legs around his waist until he's wearing me like a joey.

His firm kisses are different from yesterday. It's a good thing his members are gone, because there's no way I can keep it quiet this time. When his arms loosen, his long protrusion taunts be me on the way back to the floor. Exotic bird sounds cuckoo in the air, announcing that the house is back.

They bring us food and we devour it instead of each other.

When we finish eating, he types that he's taking me on a date. I don't have the heart to tell him that we're past all of that. Instead, I text him that I can't wait to go.

January 7

Ji volunteers to take me to my abandoned apartment after our first half of practice. My body is the leanest and strongest it's ever been from so much dancing. I would've assumed that twelve hours of practice every day was overkill until now. I don't see myself ever stopping this habit.

There isn't much to show Ji. The small apartment is clean, but not much else.

He runs his hand over the comforter on the bed and shakes his pointer finger at me.

I roll my eyes at his theater. I purposely avoided the bedroom, but he went straight inside. I need him to chase me. At least then I won't feel like such a groupie.

The restaurant he takes me to is small and cozy. Chandeliers that look like grapevines hang over the booths and tables. The decorum is white with red leather seating. The walls are white with intricate red scrawl. The tree limb design reminds me of perpetual winter.

Ji tells me the owners' story. The married couple met on Valentine's Day in America. They love Valentine's colors so much they used it to decorate. The story is a bit sappy, but Ji looks wistful while he tells it. It seems like he wants something similar. It's hard to believe it. If Ji wanted love it would be as simple as snapping his fingers. A bevy of top-notch women would be there to try out for the role. Even fellow K-Poppers lose their shit when they meet him. But, recalling the videos I've seen of him at award shows, he doesn't look phased by it all. He's always more interested in making sure he gives the fans his undivided attention.

He feeds me ramen like I'm the most important thing to him. That's what I pretend like all this is. I know it's going to end, but I've never lived out a fantasy before. If it didn't hurt so much, I could enjoy it.

He types what's wrong after I swallow down the wave of noodles on the tip of his chopsticks.

I shake my head.

He pushes his finger into the lone dimple in my cheek until I break and tell him.

[Thinking about how amazing all this is.]

[That's interesting because I was thinking about how amazing you are.]

"What?" He says.

I take his phone.

[You don't have to say that.]

[Do you not believe me?]

I want to ask him how he can think that caramel colored skin is beautiful, but I shrug instead.

[You don't have to say stuff like to get me, you've already had me.]

He licks his thumb and wipes at the corner of my mouth.

[I've had your body, but I want everything else too.]

[What do you mean everything else?]

His jaw tightens while he stares down at me. He's so intense I can't hold his gaze.

He bites his lip while he types.

[Interviewers have asked me a million times what my perfect type of woman is. I never got it right. I had never seen you.]

He fingers my chin and then pinches until I look at him. He kisses my cheek, but stops short when a sweet-faced woman visits our table.

Her magenta blushed cheeks smile at us. She points to my eyes and says something to Ji. He translates.

[She says she's never seen such beautiful eyes before.]

I ask him if he agrees with her and he shakes his head before he answers.

[That isn't what she said.] He confesses.

I nudge his solid abdomen.

[What did she say?]

[I can't tell you.]

I roll my eyes.

[First, you won't tell me what the members said, now, you won't tell me what she said. You have to tell me something.]

[No.]

I try to pout, but he pushes my bottom lip back in.

[If I told you they were both excellent things, will it please you?]

[Maybe.]

He shares his drink with me. I take a long pull on the red straw. The cocktail tastes like a mix of pineapple and cherry.

[Having a good time with me?] He types.

"Yes."

I swivel my sore neck, and he messages me. It feels too good. I try to make him stop.

[That's too good.]

He grunts something into my ear, and I scoot away from him until we're about to fall out of the U-shaped booth.

He pulls me back to the center and he hooks his leg with mine.

[Do you regret the other night?]

"Never, you?" He says confused.

"Never."

We go back to the house instead of my apartment. I'm glad he isn't hiding me, despite how much I want him. As crazy as adjusting to the grueling schedule has been, I'm comfortable at the house with the guys. They fuss over me, and it makes me feel more important than I've ever felt. I've always wanted an older brother, and out of the blue, I have six.

We go on with the evening like most every evening. He camps out in the living room joking with Woo after practice. I climb into his bed and re-play our conversations from earlier. I've gone from not knowing what the hell I was doing, to South Korea feeling like home. Despite all of the glitz and glamour in LA, there's nothing there. I've never been nor will ever be one of them. Even if my manager wasn't a lying bastard, I couldn't get used to life in

Hollywood. I've never been treated better than the guys treat me. The group looks after me more than what I called a family ever did. My mom on her best day couldn't be described as loving. The closest she ever got was funny. She wasn't much for complex emotions, but she could make me laugh until I cried. I choose to remember her like that even when the memories of her hurt.

January 26

I struggle to conceal how new this experience is when I'm in contact with Number One Management. They care about their talent. Not a day goes by that they don't check in on me. This management team not only cares that I look good, but that I feel good. In three weeks, the stylist team has my skin gleaming like a newborn's. Eun-Kyung has my longer hair laying in neat, shiny waves all styled down to the nape of my neck. I look sleek and sexy before she applies any makeup. She blends oxblood eye shadow onto my lids so well that it looks like I woke up like this. I stare at myself while she dabs at my cheeks with cinnamon-tinted blush.

"You like?"

I can't speak so I hug her. Her chubby frame holds me tight while she calls me beautiful in the best English she can come up with. I have her put my face back to its original dewy state. The last thing I want is the guys whistling at me all night. Today was prep for one of many looks Eun-Kyung will do in a few days. I like everything she does. Eun-Kyung seems so much more at ease now that she sees how much I love her work. She hands me a heavy bag full of product and then kisses my cheek before I climb into the Uber. It's always so much fun hanging out with another woman that I forget how void my life is of them now. Eun-Kyung's so good at her job, that the guys still whistle at me when I come back. I don't blame them. My skin has never looked this soft and supple. Ji doesn't like the guys giving me so much attention, but I love seeing him jealous. It like everything else looks so good on him. As far as he's concerned, I'm his, but the guys go out of their way to flirt with me just to get on his nerves.

George is due to slither into town any day. I haven't responded to any of his texts or calls since I went off on him. I'm nervous to see him again. It's one thing to be big and bad over the phone, and another to stand up to him face to face. I don't know how I'm going to stomach a twelve-hour flight sitting next to him.

As if it's possible, we practice more now that the performance is days away. We dance in restaurants. While we stand around brushing our teeth. While shopping in the city. It wouldn't surprise me if they dance on the way to the bathroom like I do. It was the funniest thing the first time they did it. Now it's second nature for me to join in when they break into a tricky part of the routine.

I've tried a million times to prepare my final dinner remarks without crying, but it's impossible. The guys have enhanced my life in ways that I didn't know I needed. I'm not only a better performer, but I'm a better person because of them.

Ji and I haven't had much alone time. Every waking second is about performance and nothing else.

He pulls me by the hand no sooner than I put my bags down. He wants me to sneak off with him to pick up breakfast. As soon as the SUV pulls off, he unzips his coat, and then mine. His body traps the heat between us, warming me better than the coat ever could. I can't believe how good his arms pressing me into his chest feels. Despite having gone much farther, this is feeding me better than any breakfast can. He doesn't let go until the SUV parks. He tells the driver to hang tight and the familiar driver says that he'll think about it. Ji threatens to steal his pillow so that he won't be able to see over the steering wheel. The driver turns the music up to drown Ji out. Ji pulls up his mask and winks at me before we exit.

I spend every free second studying Ji's language. I was too impressed with Ji's progress to not take learning Korean seriously. Now that can understand much of the Korean going on around me, it's not as interesting. I could care less about the mom threatening her toddler with no cookies if he throws his pacifier again. We have to hurry since management would kill us if they knew we were out in public like this.

"You're pretty."

I smack his hand away from my hair.

"You'll mess it up."

He threatens to touch it the whole way back.

Ji isn't shy about his feelings for me, but we keep our distance in the house.

He sings, "Bye Lei." before we go our separate ways in the foyer.

I love my stage name. Now. In LA I always felt self-conscious with such a Freudian name. But with the guys, being Lei feels exotic and mysterious.

No matter how far away Ji is in the house, he takes me with him. Even though it's much easier for us to communicate without the phones, he still shares his phone with me. Knowing that I'll have to leave him soon feels like it'll kill me. I'll never be able to do any one part of my day without thinking about him or all seven of them at the same time. It's a good thing that I've got the performance to worry about because leaving them is the last thing I want to do.

January 30

Nobody's talking today. I know why they're scared, but their silence is scaring the shit out of me. My skills are like night and day now, but it doesn't feel like there's anything I can say to make them chill out.

Nim reminds me about staying on the marks outside my dressing room. I want to tell him that I see the white X's in my dreams, but I nod and yep, careful to obey his every word.

As if I need anything else right now, George makes his grand entrance. His clothes are too tight and his cologne is too strong as usual. I still don't have anything to say to him, but he comes at me as if he owns me. Technically he does, but he doesn't have to make it so obvious.

The closer he gets the more my mouth fills with saliva. My mouth is so full when he finally reaches me that my cheeks bulge. I can't swallow because I'll blow. Jae-Hwa whistles at me when he passes my door. George eyes my cobalt, double-slit velvet jumpsuit as if he wants it for himself.

Ji doubles back when he notices George inside my dressing room. He asks George what he's doing inside my room. George spins on his heels toward the Korean words shouting at him. I race for the wastebasket and fill it up. Ji rushes inside my room and stands behind me. He rubs my back and whispers to me, all while shielding my body from George. Ji takes a break to insult George some more. Footsteps that can only be the other guys storm the room. He asks me if I'm ok before he turns around to herd everybody out. When George refuses to leave, Ji squares up and tells him to get the fuck out.

Nim sprints in front of Ji and struggles to bear hug him out the room.

Nim locks Ji in a cage, and sprints back to my door. He doesn't say anything, but the way he's wringing his hands and checking his phone every second is making me sick again. I smile at him, but he looks like he's reconsidering having me perform. He drops his manners and crosses the threshold to enter my dressing room.

"Are you cool?"

"It's just nerves."

George re-enters my room with a Sprite and I almost yak again.

Ji is back with a towel for my mouth. Instead of using it he wipes my bottom lip with a dampened thumb.

George taps his foot next Ji.

Ji turns around and scowls at George.

Nim reminds Ji that he has to let me talk to my manager.

Ji's hair falls over his brow while he swallows down his anger.

"I'll be right back to take you to makeup." He glares at George and is seconds away from throwing blows.

I squeeze his hand.

"Ji, I'm ok."

He slips a foil-wrapped tablet out of his back pocket and tells me to chew it.

I punch the pill out and take it. The second the fizzy granules break up on my tongue, I start feeling better.

Ji's out of sight, but I can feel his anger close by.

"I'm impressed by your new skill." George comments on the Korean I've been speaking since he got here. I haven't been speaking much English unless I'm talking to Nim or Ji. I only speak English with Ji in private.

It's almost insulting that he's impressed that I learned how to survive in the place he shipped me to.

"Are you ready to apologize, yet?"

Ji crosses my doorway, like a lion crossing to the other side of his cave.

I crave my toothbrush after I lick the corners of my sour mouth.

"How much am I making tonight?"

George huffs and then looks over his shoulder.

He points his swollen pointer finger at me.

"I don't know what your problem is, but I assure you that I am not it. I missed a lot of important business to come all the way here to see you perform.

"Get out."

George clenches his fists at his side.

"You do not want to do this," George says through gritted teeth.

"Do what?" Pop yells in perfect English from the door. The guys smack into each other they're running so fast to see what's up.

George ignores Pop.

"You heard her, it's time for you to go," Ji yells in English. They crowd into my room, followed by two security staff.

George wipes the sweat streaming down his temple and attempts to leave.

Pop shoulder checks him.

"Pop," Nim yells.

Security speaks into Pop's ear, and George takes the opportunity to escape.

If my exterior was the full story, I would look ready to tear up the stage. The fact is that I feel like shit inside and I won't feel better until the show is over. Win, lose or draw, anything has to be better than feeling like I'm going on stage to be burned alive. Even worse, I have a ten-minute wait until I make my entrance on the stage. There's nobody back here with me except a sound guy who looks like he should be working air traffic control. I'm under the stage hunched down on a lift. I can't see any of them, but I'm doing every step with them in my head.

When the lift has me erected in the middle of the guys I stand. The shadow of my silhouette has the audience screaming even louder. Ji stands in position in front of me.

He winks right before the beat drops and everything is quiet. I know that the music is playing but I feel it more than I hear it. Our moves are in sync, but I don't need to count the beats. Something else has taken over me, and it's nothing I can understand. All I know is that I couldn't mess this up if I wanted to.

At different moments during the performance, it almost feels too easy. Like I've become one of them. Nim introduces me in one of his raps, and he spells my name for the crowd. They lose control to hear that my name is the same as the title of one of their most popular songs.

At some point, my body reminds me that I do this for a living. The confidence that takes over makes the guys stop and watch me like they're the crowd. Performing with them makes me feel like the sexiest woman alive. The way that Ji's moves fit so well with my own style makes me glad that I didn't give up. I can finally appreciate how hard he was on me. It was the only way I could face this crowd on this stage right now.

The guys put together a montage for me that I never knew was being filmed. The jumbo screen shows the screaming crowd segments of our practices and spontaneous dancing inside of restaurants. They have footage of the museums we visited and the sites they took me to. They each take turns telling the camera why they're proud to know me. When it's Ji's turn, I can't stand up anymore. I sink down to the stage floor. His words were simple, but I heard all the things that went unspoken.

When Nim hands me the mic, I hate him for it, but no one other than the two of us can tell. Ji picks me up like a groom holding his bride, and I cry briefly into his shoulder before I recite my unrehearsed speech in the best Korean dialect I can.

"Thank you for having me tonight. I am grateful to be here tonight, performing for you. I hope I pleased you all. BIU are the best performers in the world, and I'm honored to be on this stage with them. I hope you all have a wonderful night. Seeing your beautiful faces makes me very happy. Until we meet again. So long."

The guys crowd around Ji and I, wiping at their eyes.

"You have given us the highest honor, by respecting our language and culture," Nim says.

The guys huddle in tighter to hear their leader voice what they are feeling. When they have their composure back, they unravel and bow to the crowd. Ji bows with me in his arms and doesn't put me down until the curtains scroll shut.

Dinner is somber instead of celebratory. I've always loved anything noodle related, but the colorful boxes no longer tempt me. When it's obvious that there is no good time to say goodbye, I stand up. Telling them my feelings in Korean is so much more depressing than I thought it would be. I can't get the first sentence out before every body's eyes are watering.

"First, thank you for allowing me into your home. It had to be uncomfortable having me here and having to change so much. I hope I wasn't too much of a burden on your lives."

I clear my throat. "Man-Seok, you're the funniest person I know. I smile more because I always want you to be able to see how great a person you are to me."

While we hug, I pray that I can get through all seven of them without having a nervous breakdown.

Jung-Ah sighs when Pop hands him a napkin. He's already crying, and all I've said is his name.

"You were patient with me when I wanted to give up. Your frustration must have been tested so many times going over the moves so many times. You are a generous person. I hope everyone in your life can see that." Jung-Ah clutches me tight.

"Pop you always have my back. You're always there to solve a problem, even when I least expect it. Thank you for noticing me. It's hard to find a person like you, I'm glad to know you."

His voice cracks when he tells me not to say another word. He gives me a firm squeeze and walks off. I tear up more because he's doing exactly what I envisioned him doing. Pop does not do emotions, even when he does, he's always the first one over it.

Before I start again, he's back with a present for me. It's a first edition The Old Man and The Sea by Hemingway. I have to sit down and take a few swigs of champagne to go on. I thank him and he waves me off but looks between me and the book with a proud smile on his face.

"Woo, you helped me get in the studio with confidence every day. You helped me to appreciate the full range of my voice and not only the soprano notes. I'll never be able to sing without thinking about you." Woo's been walking toward me the whole time. We're already hugging before I can finish my speech.

"Jae-Hwa, you're the mirror that shows the world how well taken care of you are. Every time you shine, you cast that light on everybody around you. I wish I was more like you. If I don't ever get there, I'll have comfort knowing that you're are the kindest person I know."

He catches Ji's eye while he comes in for a kiss. He stops short and hugs me instead. Ji's waiting for him on his way back to his seat. Ji makes it hard for him to pass, but all Jae-Hwa has to do is grin to get his way.

"Nim, you've been my compass this month from the moment I met you. You've helped me and never once asked anything in return, even when you had every right to. I hope I made you proud tonight and even better, I hope that you can call me your friend."

"Family." He says and hugs me until the guys have to shout at him to let go.

I finish my last shot of champagne. Nim fills my cup back up. I swig nothing but foam, but it doesn't matter. This never was going to be easy. Saying goodbye to Ji feels like committing suicide, but I have to do it.

The room is quiet. When I look at their expectant faces, I can't believe that I thought that professing my love for him was a good idea. There is no way in hell I can stand up in front of his members and do something so selfish. His life is with them, doing what he does best. Not coddling a woman who he had to teach how to get over herself so she could finally be of good use. He isn't looking at me. There's no doubt that he's nervous about how far I'll go in front of the group.

"Ji,"

He leaps up and hugs me one armed. He shouts a call to congratulate me for the excellent job I've done. The group doesn't hesitate to whoop and holler how proud they are. Ji hugs me and takes his seat again. Nobody questions why he cut me off and neither do I.

Everybody's finally in the mood to eat. I'm glad for the distractions because I doubt that I could've done anything less than told Ji how much I love him.

The guys threaten to kill me if I try to help clean. When I tell them that murdering me would be worse than me cleaning, Pop tells me to try it and find out.

I go to Ji's room and sit in his recliner waiting for him to finish.

He barely has the door closed when I question him.

"Why did you cut me off earlier?" I say in English.

"Because I couldn't take hearing you say such tender things. You don't understand how much you've affected them." He says in Korean.

My eyes sting. I miss them already. Especially the silver-haired man trying his best to meet my eyes right now.

"I have something to give you." He reaches in his back pocket and hands me several sheets of folded paper.

I unfold the barely folded paper and I see my name on the first line. I skip to the last page and I see George's chicken scratch on the last line underneath my signature.

"How'd you get this?"

"Your manager had to give it to me when I bought him out."

I cock my head back at his statement.

"You're free from him now. You can do anything you want in America without him leeching off of you."

I don't know whether to be happy or scared so I don't react at all. Without a manager in Hollywood, I may as well go work at McDonald's. Especially since he's on his way back to run my name into the ground.

"Shit." I curse in Korean.

Ji looks concerned and relieved that I'm speaking Korean again. I concentrate to make sure I get it right. He pulls me up off the chair, and I follow him to the bed. He wraps the covers around us before he starts explaining himself.

"I saw you on YouTube one night and I couldn't stop. I would watch you every chance I got. So much that one by one, everybody started to notice. They would tease that I'm in love with you, but I told them that I wanted to collaborate with you." He exhales a jagged breath. "I pulled some strings and got you here." He pauses for my reaction, but I'm not upset. His explanation makes more sense than George having that kind of power ever could.

"I wanted to meet you so bad that I would do anything to get you here. I came up with the whole concept of you being my muse in our comeback performance. Nim hated the idea, but the better you got the more he could finally see my vision, except it was all a lie."

I look up at him when his chest juts out.

"All I wanted was you." He says.

I lay back down on his chest. I listen to his heart pounding double time in his chest. "The more we talked about your life in LA the more I could see how much you were being abused. You were lacking the most basic things when you arrived here. Preparations that to this day you still don't know you should have had with you. I'm ashamed to hear him say that even though he's right. I never feel like I know what's going on with my supposed career.

I squeeze my eyes shut the longer he talks. His words are piercing, driving right to my core, and there's no escaping hearing what he has to say.

"They were right, and so was the woman at the restaurant. I love you, but I'll never selfishly ask you to stay here. Your life is your own to discover, and the last thing I want to be is a hindrance to you. You are a star, and everybody saw that tonight. I can't wait to see all the good things that will happen for you now that you're free to do them."

My throat feels strangled from holding back so much. I love him too but I can't make myself speak, in Korean or any other language. I don't want to be a stumbling block for him either. I want him to have the world even if I can't be in it with him.

He bends down, kisses my forehead, and slips out the bed and back to the couch.

As much as I want to beg for him to come back, I can't. It's better for the pain to start sooner rather than later. Maybe this way I can be one day closer to getting over him.

January 31

Nim gives me my first paycheck before we leave for the airport. I can't help choking when I read the amount. The guys ride as far as they can to the airport with me. Woo says that Management would kill them if they drove this far. We all laugh nervously. I understand them not being in the mood to die today. Their fans are crazy online, but in person, it's just plain scary to witness. There are troupes of them that travel around the globe to act as human barriers. They chain hands to keep rabid fans away. But these same peace keepers usually are the rabid fans.

I trade pleasantries with Ji as if my heart isn't being strangled to death. It's the one day I'm glad we're wearing masks, so that no one can see how completely messed up I am. We have to hug fast before I switch cars. Ji's black mask is high underneath his eyes when I look back at him one more time before I exit.

I ride alone for the last few miles. It's amazing how BIU has already been converted into a painful memory in my mind.

Security escorts me to the plane without incident. A small group notices me from the performance the other night. BIU's absence is the only reason the girl couldn't rally together a crazy enough group to stamped us.

The tall and friendly security staff hugs me at the gate. I still marvel at how well Number One Management has taken care of me. Security doesn't budge until I'm escorted to a first-class seat back to LA.

LA

I assumed that crying was in my immediate future when I boarded the plane, but I was wrong. The second my body had permission to stay still, I sank into a black hole.

A mild voiced flight attendant jostles me awake.

I have no sense of time or perspective while I accept the warm hand towel, she's handing me to wipe the drool off my mouth. She's so professional while she smiles down at me, unfazed at my confusion.

"Please fasten your seatbelt. We will be landing in Los Angeles shortly."

I turn over my phone and squint at the screen. It's yesterday again.

Ji's image haunting my mind makes my heart throb.

Here I was thinking that I could get a head start on getting over him, and I've got to do the whole fucking day over again.

Number One Management's last act of guardianship drives me home. It's crazy how I can have a six-figure check in my purse, but still be broke.

The bank is the first stop I plan on my way to my front door. I slow down when I see a piece of white paper taped over the peephole. I don't have to read it to know it's an eviction notice, but I torture myself anyway. If this is what he wanted me to see as soon as I arrived home, there's no telling what's next. I swallow down the shame that neighbors are snickering behind Venetian blinds. If it were not for having a check and needing to get to a bank, this situation would tip me over the edge.

It's especially hot since I have to walk three miles to the nearest bank. I haven't had an account in years, but there's no way a bank will turn down my business.

When I finally make it, my body is tight and sore. My body misses leading stretch every morning before practice. I block my mind from memories of the guys and what they're doing. Especially since I know that they're practicing. I never thought that I would long to practice hard like that again. It was pure hell until I started seeing progress. After that Ji and I were always the first ones there and the last ones to leave every day.

I park my carry-on luggage at the entrance next to the deposit slip counter. Anything to not look like a bag lady. It is not normal to pull around carry-on luggage in everyday life. I sit in one of the seats in the waiting area to soak up the air conditioner and dab the buckets of grease off my face. I'm not too scary in the mirror, but that's only because my skin has been treated so well by Eun-Yungi. I wonder how long I'll be cursed with a double mind. It has to stop. I'm already tired of correlating every second of my life back to South Korea.

I can do nothing about the dark circles under my eyes, but everything else looks decent enough. My knees and hip socket pop when I stand up to get in line for the teller. The line moves faster than I want it to for a change. I'm so nervous to hand the teller my check that I leave a slick spot on it when I slide it through the slit underneath the window.

"Good morning." She says.

"Morning."

"How can I help you today?"

"I need to cash this."

"Sure. Do you have an account with us?"

I tell her no, and her smile falters. She corrects herself quickly.

"Are you?"

I nod, hoping she'll keep it cool.

"Yeah, just got back from a performance overseas," I add in the hopes it'll add to my credibility.

"I need two forms of identification."

I slide her my license and passport, and she excuses herself to some unknown place.

When she returns a man is with her, smiling at me nervously.

"Good day Ms. Laney. We're going to need a utility bill or something with your full name and address on it."

I eye the identification he already has in his hands and tell him that I don't have that with me.

"You can understand that we need to verify your identity."

"She recognized me before I gave her my id."

"Sure, so do I. Nice to meet you, he attempts to slide his thick hand underneath the window and I squeeze at his fingers.

"Look, I'm just arriving after being away for a month. All I need is a few hundred and to deposit the rest. I can come back with anything you need after I can get into my apartment."

They look at me as confused as I sound.

"I've got to get with my landlord after being gone for so long."

They nod and look down at my check again.

"Unfortunately, without that documentation, we can't cash your check today."

I'm embarrassed but I know that there's nothing that I can do. The friendly teller slides my check back to me and mouths sorry.

A cocktail of bad emotions smacks into me on my way back to my non-existent apartment. I can't get any further than the empty back parking lot before I stop to lean against the top of my luggage. The sun is baking me, while my purse swings off my limp arm. My left arm tingles until I see that it's holding my vibrating phone.

When I answer, I recognize Ji's voice, but I don't know the voice coming out of my own mouth.

He's yelling, demanding if I'm alright. His tone is so sharp that the sound feels like it's splitting my head in two. I slide down to the hot asphalt and ask him to slow down.

He must've forgotten all the English he learned because he doesn't seem to hear me. I turn up the volume.

"Lei, where are you?"

Nim's in the background asking what's up.

I find the last of the voice coming out of me.

"Ji, I'm fine."

"Why do you sound like that?"

"Like what?"

"Like you're out of breath."

I look up at the blinding white sun and shield my eyes with an arm. My purse knocks into my eye.

"I'm, it's hot, that's all."

"Why aren't you home?"

I attempt to laugh, I sob instead.

"Lei, where are you?"

I hunch my shoulders but it doesn't sound like he saw me.

"At the bank. The trash can's back here, it smells bad."

I giggle and he's teaching me another Korean curse lesson.

I name off each curse he says, hoping that he's impressed with how hard I've been studying.

"You sound bad. Go home."

"I don't have one. Lovely Georgie kicked me out."

"Lei," Ji yells like a drill sergeant. "Map your location and give me the coordinates.

"Yes, sir."

I salute and do as he says. My fingers shake and slip off the phone screen, but I know to obey him, or I'll have to dance forever today.

"Stay on the phone with me until an Uber picks you up."

"Ok, I'll just sleep right here for a second." I push my luggage over and lay on top of it. My skin screams as it burns under the direct sunlight but I pretend that it's a heated blanket and that it's snowing.

Someone's picking me up off the ground, and I try to fight for my life, but it's no use. The man is strong. So strong that he picks me up and puts me in the car. He explains to me that he has explicit instructions to get me to the plane. When he says my name, I remember him dropping me off earlier. I cry into his shoulder.

He tells me that I'll be ok now, just rest until he can get me back to South Korea.

South Korea

I can take Ji being upset with me. After my childhood, there isn't much that I haven't seen or heard. But what I can't take is how he goes out of his way to make me know it. He has the whole house on edge the way he barks at anybody trying to come in his room to talk to me.

I haven't been back to South Korea for two hours, but it feels like I never left. If it were not for my half scathed, half sunburned body, I could shelve LA away like all my other nightmares.

When Ji has my clothes unpacked and there's nothing else to distract himself with, he faces me.

"Why didn't you tell me that things were so bad back home?"

Hearing him speak to me again sounds so good I don't want to answer.

"You had plenty of money to take care of things, why didn't you just deposit the money you earned?"

I look at him and beg him to stop silently.

"There's got to be somebody you could've gone to."

I pull my mask up higher, even though my vision is already obscured by the tears brimming.

"If this is how you act when I've asked you for nothing. How will you act when I do?" I ask in Korean.

Ji doesn't blink. He doesn't move. It's hard to know that he's still breathing he's so quiet.

"I would do anything to help you. I love..."

I rip off my mask.

"Anything but keep me from leaving."

"This is not my fault, Lei. I want the best for you."

"How would you know what's the best for me?"

He sits down next to me and reaches for my hand but I snatch it away.

I don't want to do this, especially with him. None of this is what he deserves, but I can't bottle this shit up another second.

"I love you. I wanted to tell you that, but you wouldn't let me. I know you have a life. I wasn't going to ask you to be with me." I say.

He scoots close enough to wipe my tears. I roll my head to dodge him, but I'm too exhausted to get away.

"I never expected for you to be ok with me intruding on your life." I say.

"Intrude on me, Lei."

He can't mean what he's saying. I suck my dry lips inside my mouth to block his kisses but he persists until my mouth shakes from the effort.

"I didn't know for sure if you loved me as I love you." He says.

It hurts when I scrunch my face.

"Stop it." He stops kissing me until I do. "Yes, I held back the truth from you, but only because I didn't want you to think I was trying to manipulate you."

"Manipulate me."

Epilogue

Number One Management signs me. I am not a member of BIU. All parties agree that we're better off as separate acts. We can collaborate whenever we choose to. The guys force me to look at our performance online. Now I understand why Number One Management signed me. They had to. The fans threatened to riot if they didn't bring me back.

Not much about our lives in Korea changes. We practice every day until someone falls out on the floor gasping for breath. We eat until we feel fat and then we dance it back off. We wake up to the same thing every day and it's exactly what I want.

Number One Management moves me into a cozy house across the street from the guys, but Ji is there every morning. He creeps over every night like no one knows he's here. Practice is harder since we rarely get enough sleep, but it's worth it. All of this is worth it. The cancer air, sneaking to public places without permission, dancing in public. Living in a foreign country away from everything that's familiar to me can't be better for my life. It is all worth it to have Ji whispering to me in Korean at night. Except it's even better because now can tell him how much I love him back.

More By, T.A. Walker

Bad On Paper
Ex
Love Chronicles:
Niccolo (Pt.1)
Niccola (Pt. 2)
Lina (Pt.3)

Thank you for your valuable time. I hope that it was time well spent. All of the above digital titles are free, and will remain so as a thank you to all who enjoy my work. Please be sure to follow my Amazon page to get notifications whenever there's a new release.
Cheers!
T.A. Walker

Made in the USA
Monee, IL
25 February 2024

54094582R00035